The Giant
Jumperee

For Josephine Julia – J. D.

For Lily – H. O.

PUFFIN BOOKS
UK | USA | Canada | Ireland | Australia | India | New Zealand | South Africa
Puffin Books is part of the Penguin Random House group of companies
whose addresses can be found at global.penguinrandomhouse.com.
www.penguin.co.uk   www.puffin.co.uk   www.ladybird.co.uk

Penguin
Random House
UK

First published as a picture book 2017
Based on *The Giant Jumperee* play, written by Julia Donaldson
and published in the Pearson Rigby Star series in 2000
001
Text copyright © Julia Donaldson, 2017
Illustrations copyright © Helen Oxenbury, 2017
The moral right of the author and illustrator has been asserted
Printed in China
A CIP catalogue record for this book is available from the British Library
ISBN: 978-0-141-36382-0
All correspondence to: Puffin Books, Penguin Random House Children's, 80 Strand, London WC2R 0RL

The Giant Jumperee

written by

JULIA DONALDSON

illustrated by

HELEN OXENBURY

PUFFIN

Rabbit was hopping home one day when he heard
a loud voice coming from inside his burrow.

"I'm the
GIANT JUMPEREE
and I'm scary
as can be!"

"Help! Help!" cried Rabbit.

"What's the matter, Rabbit?" asked Cat.

"There's a Giant Jumperee in
my burrow!" said Rabbit.

"Don't worry," said Cat.
"I'll slink inside and pounce on him!"

So Cat slunk up to the burrow.

But just as she was about to slink inside
she heard a loud voice.

"I'm the
GIANT JUMPEREE
and I'll squash you
like a flea!"

"Help! Help!" miaowed Cat.

"What's the matter, Cat?" asked Bear.

"There's a Giant Jumperee in
Rabbit's burrow!" said Cat.

"Don't worry," said Bear. "I'll put my
big furry paw inside and knock him down."

So Bear swaggered up to the burrow.
But just as he put his big furry paw
inside he heard a loud voice.

"I'm the
GIANT JUMPEREE
and I'll sting you
like a bee!"

"Help! Help!" bellowed Bear.

"What's the matter, Bear?" asked Elephant.

"There's a Giant Jumperee in
Rabbit's burrow!" said Bear.

"Don't worry," said Elephant. "I'll wrap my trunk round him and toss him away."

So Elephant stomped up to the burrow.
But just as he put his long grey trunk
inside he heard a loud voice.

"I'm the
GIANT JUMPEREE
and I'm taller
than a tree!"

"Help! Help!" trumpeted Elephant.

"What's the matter, Elephant?" asked Mummy Frog.

"There's a Giant Jumperee in
Rabbit's burrow!" said Elephant.

"Don't worry," said Mummy Frog.
"I'll tell him to come out."

"No, no! Don't do that!" said all the other animals.

"He's as scary as can be," said Rabbit.

"He can squash you like
a flea," said Cat.

"He can sting you like a bee," said Bear.

"And he's taller than a tree," said Elephant.

But Mummy Frog took
no notice of them.

She jumped up to the burrow.

"I'm the
GIANT JUMPEREE
and you're terrified
of me!"

came the loud voice.

The other animals backed away.

But Mummy Frog wasn't scared.

"Come on out,

GIANT JUMPEREE!" she said.
"You're the one we want to see,
so I'm counting
up to three!

"One . . .

two . . .

THREE!"

Then out jumped . . .

. . . Baby Frog!

"Hello, Mum! I'm the GIANT JUMPEREE!"

"And you're coming home to tea!"
said Mummy Frog.